Anonymous

The Three Little Kittens

Anonymous

The Three Little Kittens

ISBN/EAN: 9783744642286

Hergestellt in Europa, USA, Kanada, Australien, Japan

Cover: Foto ©Andreas Hilbeck / pixelio.de

Weitere Bücher finden Sie auf **www.hansebooks.com**

THE THREE LITTLE KITTENS
AND THEIR MITTENS

THREE little kittens,
 They lost their mittens,
 And they began to cry,
 "Oh! mammy dear, we sadly fear,
Our mittens we have lost!"
 "What! lost your mittens,
You naughty kittens!
 Then you shall have no pie."
 Miew, miew, miew, miew,
 Miew, miew, miew, miew.

The Three Little Kittens.

The three little kittens
Had need of mittens;
 The winter now was nigh.
"Oh! mammy dear, we fear, we fear,
 Our mittens we shall need."
"Go, seek your mittens,
You silly kittens!
 There's tempest in the sky."
  Miew, miew, miew, miew,
  Miew, miew, miew, miew.

The Three Little Kittens.

The three little kittens,
In seeking their mittens,
    Upset the table high.
"Oh! mammy dear, we doubt and fear,
  The house is tumbling down."
"You foolish kittens!
Go, find your mittens,
    And do not make things fly."
        Miew, miew, miew, miew,
        Miew, miew, miew, miew.

The three little kittens,
They found their mittens,
    And they began to cry,
"Oh! mammy dear, see here, see here,
 Our mittens we have found."
"What! found your mittens,
You little kittens,
    Then you shall have some pie."
        Purr, purr, purr, purr,
        Purr, purr, purr, purr.

The Three Little Kittens.

The three little kittens,
Put on their mittens.
    And soon ate up the pie!
"Oh! mammy dear, we greatly fear,
    Our mittens we have soiled."
"What! soiled your mittens,
You naughty kittens!"
    Then they began to sigh,
        Miew, miew, miew, miew,
        Miew, miew, miew, miew.

The Three Little Kittens.

The three little kittens,
They washed their mittens,
    And hung them up to dry
    "Oh! mammy dear, look here, look here,
Our mittens we have washed."
    "What! washed your mittens,
You darling kittens!
    But I smell a rat close by!
        Hush! hush!" Miew, miew,
        Miew, miew, miew, miew.